2

There are so many people I would like to thank for "saving" me. To all of you that have supported my blog all these years, this book is for you.

Many special thanks to Kate Scott!

For My Friend Giovanni Macchia, For reminding Me that My Story is about More than Just a Simple bear.

AND FOR Kathy Williams ☺

CHapter 1

I think I'd like to tell you a very simple story about bravery. Heroes do come in all shapes and sizes, we all know that. But, do you know that bravery also takes on very different forms? You may think of bravery as a thing only for the strong and mighty, with their swords and shields, but sometimes something as simple as a smile can be brave.

I realize while telling you this story that there might be words you do not know, or have not heard before, or may find hard to pronounce. I had thought about leaving them out, but then I realized that you were smarter than that. You deserve big words when they are necessary, because I know that you can handle them. If you come across a word you don't understand, find yourself a dictionary, learn what it means, and you'll be one word smarter than your friends every time you do so.

I had also thought that I'd put in pictures or elaborate drawings, but then I thought again, you were much too smart for that. Your imagination will do you much better than any drawing I could ever come up with, and using your imagination is very important. There are so many things you can accomplish in life when your imagination is allowed to flourish. So, instead of putting in this story all sorts of detailed drawings, I only scribbled a few doodles, just for my own enjoyment. ☺

So, sit back, relax and let me tell you all about a very small teddy bear.

Deep in the thick quiet woods, far from the many busy bodies and noisy cars of the city, lived a young boy named Jackson. Cozy and tucked in a small wood framed house, nestled amongst so many large and valiant old trees, Jackson lived with his father, whom he simply called "Dad."

They had not always lived in this quaint house. They used to live in the city, in a tall apartment building with only one window to look out of, and the view was always grey and dismal. The apartment was so high in the sky that sometimes you couldn't even see the street below, for the air was filled with thick, heavy clouds of smog. And once you were down on the street things weren't so much better. The city was colorless, devoid of trees, with so many people rushing about, stomping on you sometimes as they hurried by.

Jackson had been taught by his parents some very good manners. He was always to be polite, to be kind always, respectful to everyone, and to always say, "Please" and "Thank you." However, he never understood how so many people could be so rude. For instance, with him being such a small boy, he wondered why the adults would nearly trample on him as he walked down the avenues on his way to school without the first one of them saying, "Excuse me, I'm sorry."

Why, if he had nearly stepped on someone and had not at least said "Excuse me," his parents would have properly scolded him. His favorite television show would be banned for a week, his favorite after school activities would be suspended. But, alas, that was life in the city, his Dad often said. "People here don't see other people around them. It's funny," he'd say, "that with all these people it can still be so lonely."

Jackson's Dad was a peculiar man, for though he worked and spent tireless hours working in the city, he yearned especially for the noble greatness of the forest, with all of it's animals, it's shimmering bugs, it's golden rays that pierced the limbs of the mighty oaks, and shed light on the moss of the earth.

When Dad wasn't working, he was always building something, or making something, or creating something. He once built Jackson a small wooden chair, just the right size to sit and watch his favorite show on television. No longer would Jackson have to climb the heights of the couch, then get swallowed up by the cushions. He now had his own chair, perfectly suited for his little body.

Jackson was very much like his father. He used to look out their one window and pout, also dreaming of a faraway place where things grew naturally out of the ground. Out of that window he would day dream of catching fireflies and chasing wrens as they flew through an open meadow of speckled green.

Jackson's mother, however, was not at all interested in dirt and bugs and smelly animals. She preferred the tightly constrained life of the city. She loved the skyscrapers, loved the noise of the streets bustling with energy, and the hurried rush to always be somewhere. That made you important in her mind. She thought that if you looked busy and in a hurry, that people thought you were important, that you were greatly needed somewhere at once. So

Mom always dashed here, swiftly darted there, and all the while with no real place to go.

To be plain and simple, Dad wanted things…..well, plain and simple. And Mom wanted things extravagant and loud.

Naturally, with Mom and Dad seeing so many things differently in the world, there were often disagreements and arguments. Which is why Jackson would often sit at that window and pout. It wasn't because he was being selfish, he was just lonely and confused. Home should be where you come to everyday and feel love and inclusion. But, he didn't live in a home, he lived in an apartment where Mom and Dad were often angry, where if there weren't arguments, there were eerie quiet times where you knew no one was speaking to each other because no one liked each other.

Now, don't get me wrong, by all means. Jackson loved both of his parents equally. He just couldn't understand why Mom and Dad didn't love each other equally also.

Jackson had very few friends at school. But, that was ok, because he had a little knit teddy bear his father had made for him. Of course, he clutched his prized bear all the time, and took it with him everywhere. It reminded him of two things during those days. The first is that he would never be alone. He always had his teddy bear to keep him company, to talk to when no one was speaking to each other, to watch television with when Mom was busy rushing somewhere, and Dad was busy being creative. The second thing it reminded him of was that his Dad had knit it with his own two hands *just for him*, and that made the teddy bear very, *very* special.

I know you might think it odd that his father had knit him the teddy bear. After all, when many people think of knitting, they do think of little old grandmas sitting in rocking chairs and making shawls to keep themselves warm in summer. I completely understand why you think that way, but I have to tell you that all kinds of people knit; boys and girls, big and small, old and young. You see, creative people find different ways to make things and express their feelings, and knitting is really no different. So Dad, knowing how lonely and sad Jackson was, knit a little bear for him just so he would always know that his father loved him and that he would never be alone.

Sadly, the day did come when Jackson was asked by his parents if he would rather live in the city or perhaps out in the woods.

Mom and Dad were sitting on the couch, but at opposite sides facing Jackson, who sit in the clever chair Dad had made.

Mom made her case: "There are so many things to do, so many places to go, so many things to see in the city!"

And Dad made his case: "But, you could run through the woods, build things, and rest when you want under a shady old tree."

Now, they never told Jackson why they were asking him such an odd question, so he just blurted out as fast as he could, "THE FOREST! YEAH! I want to live in the forest! Are there snakes out there?"

"Yes! Far too many of them," shouted his mother.

"Good!" Replied Jackson.

And thus the deal was sealed, as they say. Jackson's mother lowered her head and looked to the floor. Noticing her sadness, Jackson asked, "What's wrong, Mom?"

Holding back tears she said, "Your father and I are going to live separately for a while. He's going to move out to the woods and I'm going to stay here.

We just wanted to know where you would be happiest before we told you."

That didn't make things any better for Jackson. His heart sank, for he felt he had hurt his mother. He might have given a different answer if he had known the nature of the question, wouldn't he? Who knows? But, for the moment, he had stated loudly that he wanted to live in the woods....with his father, which truly must have hurt his mother deeply.

Feeling so terrible, he grabbed his teddy bear, clutched him tight and went to his room and cried.

Chapter 2

Moving to the woods was at first rocky and difficult for Jackson. He hated leaving his mother behind, but was reminded by his father that he would see her often.

However, there was *soooo* many distractions once he was out in the clean air and sunlight. He saw whimsical bugs float atop flower petals, watched rabbits dash quickly through the thick meadow, heard birds cry for affection, and baby deer run for protection.

He made friends quite fast with the other children that went to his school, all of them also living in the woods, each of them inviting him to go fishing, or to catch frogs, or to build forts with fallen tree limbs. Jackson fell in love with living in the woods. It was the perfect life for an imaginative little boy.

That little wood framed house became creative and wonderful to him. The sun always shined, and there were windows in every room, but who needed them when you could go outside???

He would run with his friends through the spurs, then pluck them off his pant legs as they sat by the creek; would lay on their backs and watch the clouds and give them stories, rather than say what they looked like. "That cloud's name is," said Jackson one day, "brave Indian chief defending his fortress...."

"Oh, yeah? Well, that cloud," replied his friend, "is a princess escaping the wrath of an evil queen."

His mind was allowed to soar, his explorations were allowed to blossom, and his new friends made him feel welcome.

Jackson and his Dad had not brought a television with them, nor a radio, or anything like that into the woods. When they were together in the evening they would read books, tell stories, or make things. Dad started knitting Jackson a whole new army of animals, a new squadron of vicious and exotic creatures to keep him and his teddy bear company.

First their was a fierce tiger that Jackson simply called, "The fanged warrior that fights off evil enemies," not realizing that sometimes tigers are simply for cuddling. However, not long after, he soon lost him.

"I think he was stolen," Jackson protested.

Then Dad knit him an elephant that Jackson soon named, "the largest beast of the jungle so large it can take down a tree with one stomp," not realizing that elephants would rather be studious, and educated, and read a lot. There then came a rabbit made with all sorts of different colors.

Jackson asked why the rabbit looked like that and Dad replied, "He's wearing war paint." Jackson didn't realize that Dad had run out of yarn for the proper color of a rabbit, so he used yarn left over from other things. Finally, Dad knit Jackson a very noble lion, "that can roar so loud the flowers in the field curl away in terror!"

Life in the woods was beautiful, simple and pure as Dad had always wanted; adventurous and fun, as Jackson had always hoped for.

However, don't think for a moment that Jackson didn't agonize over the fact that his parents were now separated, living different lives, and perhaps that is what made Jackson sick.

With all the shiny things that can distract you from your feelings, you can forget being heartbroken. And sometimes being heartbroken can cause just as much illness as a sneeze.

It wasn't but a few months after being out in the woods that Jackson became very ill, so ill he was forced into bed and slept an awful lot. At first you might think this was a lot of fun. After all, who doesn't like the idea of staying home from school, of getting to stay in bed and read comic books, of getting to play with your toys all day?

But, soon it became apparent that Jackson wasn't interested in those things. He longed to be at school with his friends, to be out in the forest building tree houses and digging imaginary canals, and most of all, having fun.

Being in bed was boring, but it didn't matter so much, for his illness got so bad so fast that he simply was too weak to do anything other than sleep. Jackson was hardly aware of what was going on around him. He had kept his teddy bear close the whole time, never let him out of sight, never stopped cuddling him….

He didn't realize the little bear's stuffing was coming out the seams, had started to split open, that one of his eyes had started to come undone, that one of his ears looked like it had been nibbled away….until one day Jackson woke groggily to find his teddy bear was gone.

He moaned softly from the bed for his father. "I think someone stole my teddy bear…"

"No, son. No one stole your teddy bear."

"Then where is he?"

"He's…..he's in the living room getting all patched up."

"Is he ok?"

"He'll be just fine. Now, go back to bed and get some sleep."

"But, I don't know if I can sleep without him with me."

"He'll be back in no time."

CHapter 3

I'm not sure if you're aware of this, but all hand made toys are made with magic. Oh, sure, they might be knit with wool, and stuffed with plush, but the real secret is magic. Hands might create things with love and care, but it is the heart that creates magic. And all things made with magic have a purpose, and every hand knit toy knows this. However, sometimes knitted things have a hard time figuring out what their purpose is.

Dad wasn't patching up his old teddy bear, for the poor little thing just could not be rescued and was beyond repair. Instead, he knit Jackson a new and improved bear, knitting him all day and deep into the early evening, his fingers carefully knitting the bear with love and care, but his heart knitting it with unseen magic.

Every once in a while Dad would lay the knitting to his side, rise from his giant, comfortable chair and walk a few steps to Jackson's room.

Peeking through the door he could see the soft rays of the sun streak through the slits in the closed blinds to rest on the poor boy's small face. His breathing was heavy and hard, his skin quite pale, and the damp from his fever wet his pajama top. But, snuggled under the bed he should stay.

"Poor thing," Dad whispered to himself, and as though it were a reminder of how important his knitting was, quickly went back to his yarn to finish his project.

Just when it was too dark to see, at just the point the light in the room went grey, the teddy bear was complete. With some sewing here, tucking there, and embroidering quaint little eyes above his muzzle, the soft thing was finally finished and ready to give. Dad said with a smile, "This is JUST what Jackson needs to make him feel better."

He didn't dare wake Jackson while he slept. Rest was the best medicine for the moment, the only thing that worked. Jackson's sad illness was draining so much from him. So, Dad let Jackson sleep, and tenderly set the teddy bear beside him in bed.

When Jackson woke the next morning, he made his usual grimaces. We all hate mornings, but Jackson's were often different than many of ours. He would wake with a slight shake in his face, a twist in his brow, a heavy sigh. Mornings meant medicine, lots of medicine, so much horrible tasting medicine that his lips would pierce just thinking about it.

As he rolled over in bed he saw a new little teddy bear just quietly sitting there beside him. Jackson clutched him with glee, holding him close to his chest, forgetting all about the medicine.

As Dad came in to bring Jackson's morning tray of medicine, he found the boy squeezing the knit teddy bear close to his chest, sitting upright in bed with a cheerful grin.

"Hey, little man," Dad said laughing, "it's been a long time since I've seen you smile! Do you like him?"

Jackson asked anxiously, "Where is my other bear?"

"Your other bear knows how sick you've been and he knew he needed some extra help to get you feeling better, so this guy showed up."

"Where do you think he came from?"

"I don't know," he said so happy to see his child finally in good spirits. "He was probably roaming around the woods and heard there was a little boy in need of some company."

"Who do you think told him?"

"Probably the rabbits. You know they like to gossip. They run around the fields and meadows twitching their little noses and spreading news. My guess is your other bear was spreading word out in the woods that you needed help. The rabbits probably heard the news and started telling all the other animals that a very special bear was needed here."

Jackson squeezed the little bear even tighter and said, "I sure am glad he came."

"What are you going to call him?"

"Hmmmm. I haven't decided...."

"I think this one is special. He deserves a special name."

"Well, what do you think I should call him?"

"What does your heart tell you?"

Jackson paused, looked at the little bear for an awfully long time, and as if looking into his eyes said, "The little sick boy's bear." There came the pout, the bear slowly lowered to his lap, Jackson's face drawing scared.

Dad held him quickly. "Jackson, we're going to make you well again. I promise. We're going to do everything we can." And even Dad was trying his best to believe it, too. "Don't name him just yet.

Name him when you feel it's right. When the name just pops into your heart, not into your head. And call him whatever you want."

"Can I call him 'Fearless Lord Crocodile Killer?'"

Dad giggled and said, "If that's truly what your heart tells you, then yes. By all means.....but, remember, only if that's what your heart tells you."

Jackson had his shy morning breakfast. A simple piece of toast, a fried egg, a glass of juice, and spoonful after spoonful of the most repulsive medicine you could have ever imagined. It tasted like how the bottom of his fishing box smelled and looked like the muddy edge of the creek he threw stones in.

Soon after, Jackson grew drowsy as the medicine began doing its work. He gently laid on his back, brought the little teddy bear to his chest, Jackson's labored breathe lifting and dropping the little bear's head in a comforting rhythm as he slowly went to sleep.

And that, my friends, is when the magic began....

Chapter 4

The little bear gradually, and every so cautiously, lifted his head so he wouldn't disturb Jackson. He sniffed the sleeping boy, as bears often do.

"Oh, no," the bear whispered. "He's sick. Really sick."

He silently pulled his paws off of Jackson, but with just a little rustle of the boy's movement, the bear went limp and fell back into place. When he thought Jackson had gone back to sleep again, the bear rose and sat at the edge of the bed looking tenderly back.

"That's so sad," said the little bear shaking his head. Suddenly, Jackson rolled over with a groan, his scrawny arm grabbing the little bear and pulling him tightly against his chest.

"OOOMPH!" exclaimed the little bear as quietly as he could.

Twisting his mouth a little he thought, "I could stay here for a moment. Yes, I could just lay here for a moment….but, I would rather be doing something to help him. I need to do *something*. Isn't that why I'm here? To help him?"

Finally, he said it out loud. "I wish I knew what was wrong with him."

It sounded like the growl of an approaching thunder storm: a deep, rolling voice heard in the corner of the room that startled the little bear. "He's sick," the voice said.

"Who said that?"

"I did." Oh, and what a voice it was, the kind that causes the timber of the woods to tremble.

"Who are you?"

"Who are *you*?" Asked the voice in return.

The little bear stopped for a moment before realizing the only answer he could give was the truth. "He didn't give me a name yet."

"No name, you say?"

"Nope. You said the boy was sick?"

"Yes. He's been sick for a long while…." Out from the shadows stepped with regal perfection and heroic stroll, a knit lion….. "And he doesn't seem to be getting any better."

The little bear was stunned at the sight. He was orange and majestic, with a big brown crown of a mane that proved how important he was. And the way he glided across the room towards the little bear showed remarkable grace.

"Wow…," was all the little bear could say under his little breath.

"My name is *'the lion that can roar so loud the flowers in the field curl away in terror.'"* The lion stood proud before the little bear.

"I believe you!" Said the little bear.

And if lions could smile, this one would have. But, lions are serious and stern. Smiling can sometimes make their snouts ache.

"But, you can just can me 'lion.'"

The little bear, slightly intimidated by the lion's presence had a thought.

"How could the boy get sick with YOU around? Can't you scare away the illness?"

"I can't roar and chase his illness away. It doesn't work like that." The lion's long tale swung around with a gliding ease to rest before him.

"Well, if *you* can't do something, maybe I can. I can at least *try* to do something. ANYTHING!" The little bear said this while trying to wrestle his way out of Jackson's grasp.

"If you keep squirming like that, he'll wake up. He needs to rest, so you wouldn't be helping him very much."

"How do I get out so I can help him?"

"Maybe I can assist you." The lion took a deep breath, closed his eyes, his chest expanding mightily and grand, and the little bear just knew he was about to hear the roar of a lifetime, a roar so penetrating and deep that the little bears stuffing might shake. Instead, the lion just growled....It was a soft and steady growl, but by no means simple.

Suddenly, Jackson took a deep breath of his own, rolled over, letting the little bear go, and with a sigh, went back to sleep on his other side.

The lion slowly wandered to the other side of the bed and said in Jackson's sad ear, "Stay brave, little one."

The little bear looked at the lion inquisitively. "What did you mean by that?"

"A roar can't chase away an illness. But, bravery can. As long as he stays brave, he can fight this and win. That's why I'm here. *That* is why I am a lion. Dad made me to remind the boy to stay brave in any battle he might face. I stand here never ceasing in my duty. You don't need a lot of noise to remind someone to be brave. Sometimes a little growl does the trick. Look at how he's sleeping now. Somewhere in his little heart he's fighting his illness with bravery. Somewhere in his dreams, he is a proud warrior fending off pain."

The lion lifted his chin, so proud of his work, so steadfastly impressed at how well Dad had knit him. "It's all I can do, but I promise you little bear, it is the what I was *made* to do."

So touched, so heartfelt, the little bear said with absolute certainty, "I think I can do something, too. I just don't know what that is."

"We shall see, little bear, we shall see. Everyone is made for a reason. Your reason will shine in time."

CHapter 5

The lion asked, "Now that you are free, little bear, what are you going to do to help him?"

The little bear couldn't think of anything. His heart was filled, of course, with a need to help Jackson, but somehow he couldn't make those feelings into words that made sense to the lion.

Do you ever have that feeling? You can't say the words, but you know your heart is loudly, proudly, shouting precisely what it should be?

The little bear stumbled and stuttered, "Well, because...... it's like this.... I want to.....shouldn't I? I don't know....it's just a feeling that I have to do *something* to help him."

Just then, the little bear heard a faint flapping sound in the corner. The lion's gaze shifted quickly to that direction. His keen perceiving ears twisted toward the noise.

The little bear lowered his voice. "What was that?"

There it was again.

Flappthhhh. Flapppitty flapppth!!!

No! Wait! Now he could hear it a *third* time. This strange *flippity flappity flufpity* noise floating through the air.

"Quickly," said the lion in a hush, "under the covers! GO! NOW!"

The little bear did as he was told, the lion rushing under the bed and whispering in that deep tone of his that reverberated the room, "Don't make a noise. Stay quiet and hidden. Do you understand, little bear? Don't let them see you!"

"Who???"

"The Moths...."

The little bear peeked from out of the covers to see a dainty little moth dance rapidly through the sunbeams in the room. He landed there for a moment, then over here for a second, then flightily dashed all over the room.

The little bear asked the lion what that was. "It's so strange, so small, why are we hiding from it?"

"Oh, you have much to learn, little bear. That's a Moth. He's not alone, either. There are many of them out there. They like this time of day. They love flying wildly in the sunlight."

"Why should I be afraid of something so small?"

"Because he, my friend, can eat you alive."

The little bear was amazed at the Moth's glowing wings rapidly flapping with such a speed. They looked like spinning jewels. The delicate thing would bounce and flutter, dashing through the room, never quite pleased at what it had seen.

"He's looking for us," the lion growled.

"Why us?"

"Because the Moths love to feed on knitted things."

"Can't you roar and make him go away?"

"Oh, no. I don't want him to know I'm here either."

"I thought you said you were brave."

"Knowing the truth is brave, little bear, and the truth is, he can have us for dinner. I lost a good friend to the Moths the last time they were here. I shall not lose another."

The little bear cowered under the blanket, pulling the cover over his head and curling close to Jackson's body. "Let me know when he's gone," said the little bear.

The Moth then flew closer to the blanket, hovering just above where the little bear was hiding. Resting in mid air, it's elegant wings flittering so quickly, it simply stared at the piled mound of blanket where the little bear recoiled with fear.

Poof!

Suddenly the Moth was gone, dashing out of the room, back out of the window and into the glaring sun, but not before reeling itself back in one last time to take a second look....

Chapter 6

There was a subtle rustle in the closet, then suddenly the faintest whisper, *"Psst, hey!....PSSSSST! LION! PSSST PSST!"*

The little bear's eyes began to widen and as the lion crept from underneath the bed. Again the frail voice in the closet whispered with a raspy, *"Hey, lion! Is it safe to come out?"*

"For the moment," responded the lion.

Now, from out of the closet, from under a pile of clothes and toys, a rabbit appeared. But, this rabbit wasn't like the ones you usually see. You imagine them to be brown, or tan, or maybe a little grey, but this bunny was different colors, unusual colors for a rabbit. He had been knit up in different stripes of purple and blue, and a hint of pink around his face. Each of his long ears were also a different color, as one flopped forward, the other falling back behind his head.

You might also imagine that rabbits and bunnies are usually bouncing and hopping here and there. But, this rabbit did no such thing. As a matter of fact, he lurked slowly out of the closet, calmly stepped one leg at a time to the edge of the bed where the lion awaited him. He motioned for the lion to come closer: "I don't want to spread rumors, but is it safe for the others to come out now, too?"

You know how rabbits can be. Despite this being no ordinary looking rabbit, he still had a rabbit's heart, and did best what rabbit's do: they love to spread stories. They love to run from glen to glen telling everyone what they've seen or heard. One rabbit tells another, then that rabbit tells his friends. The next thing you now, you have a chatterbox of bunnies out in the forest, all spreading rumors and only sometimes truths.

The lion proudly said, "Yes, you can tell the others that all is safe for the moment."

The rabbit quickly looked left, quickly looked right and put his little paw over his mouth before asking, " What about this guy, the new bear, is he ok?"

"Perfectly."

The rabbit slowly turned around and went back into the closet. And oh, what a mess that closet was. It was totally disorganized and frightfully full of stuff. And yes, I do mean *STUFF*. Anything and everything a little boy might have was tossed in there.

Unfortunately, before Jackson had taken ill, he had fallen into that same trap that many young boys and girls are lured by. I call it, "The Invisible Chamber of Dirty Clothes and Secrets." I'm sure you know what I mean.

When asked by your parents to make your room tidy, many boys and girls cleverly employ "The Invisible Chamber of Dirty Clothes and Secrets" technique. Nothing gets put where it's supposed to go, but everything gets shuffled into a pile in one of two places: under the bed, or in the closet.

The closet is the best example, for you can throw everything and anything in there, cram it tight, then shut the door behind and *poof!* All of your dirty clothes and secrets become invisible. No one can see them. Dirty clothes, old homework assignments, all sorts of things get thrown into the closet to make it seem as though your room were clean.

Seems like a worthwhile trick, doesn't it? Sadly, it is not. For while you are cramming your closet with things that you picked up off the floor just to give the illusion of tidiness, you have a tendency to pick up your favorite things, too. Like some of your favorite toys. And like anyone else, those things once thrown in the closet become invisible even to you. Some things you want to forget, but some things get accidentally thrown in, too. And that's the bad part about having an "Invisible Chamber of Dirty Clothes and Secrets." Good things go unnoticed, too. Like Jackson's tiger.

Do you remember my telling you that Jackson's beloved tiger went missing? How

Jackson thought someone had stolen him? Well, this is how it happened.

One day, Jackson was wearing a very nice shirt his dad had bought for him. Now, Jackson had been warned on more than one occasion, that if he wanted to play with his friends, he was take the shirt off and wear a different one. This shirt was never to be ruined. But, not thinking of the shirt, and only wanting to play, Jackson forgot the rule and spent a great afternoon running through the woods, helping to build a fort out of fallen timber, and splashing through the little creek that edged where they lived.

But, once he got home and was getting ready for dinner, he saw while taking his shirt off this enormous rip right up the side. It wasn't a simple tear, my friend, but this *HUGE* gaping hole. The shirt fell to the floor just as Jackson's Dad was calling for him.

"Jackson? Did you clean your room? I'll be up in five minutes to check." Jackson quickly raced around the room, first picking up the shirt, then everything else that made the room messy. He bundled everything up into one pile and threw it into the closet. Just then, Jackson's dad opened the door and said, "Dinner's ready. Your room looks good. Keep it up!"

But, what Jackson didn't realize is that his shirt had fallen on his friendly tiger, and when he scooped up the shirt, he had also scooped up his friend, tossing him into "The Invisible Chamber of Dirty Clothes and Secrets."

A few days later, Jackson was in a panic, and couldn't find his tiger. "I've looked everywhere! Someone stole my tiger!"

Now, we could talk for a minute about how sad Jackson was that he lost his friend, but I think it would be better to really talk about how the tiger felt. He was heartbroken. That's the easiest way to say it, isn't it? How do you think the tiger felt? He was trapped under a pile of all the things Jackson wanted to get rid of, or hide, and all the while the tiger felt he had been dismissed and rejected by his friend. To make matter worse, once Jackson realized that his tiger was gone, he *DID* go through the closet and began rummaging through everything to find him. But, sadly, the tiger kept slipping through clothes that Jackson had discarded, falling between jeans that were muddy, and shirts that were torn until finally, the tiger was at the bottom of the heap. Jackson never found him. And the tiger stayed there as Jackson piled more and more things into the closet that he wanted to forget.

Feeling unloved is a horrible thing, especially when it's a misunderstanding. Jackson didn't mean to toss away his tiger, no more than he meant to hurt his own Mom's feelings, but the tiger didn't know that. This is why having an "Invisible Chamber of Dirty Clothes and Secrets" is not always a good idea. Sometimes, good things are accidentally forgotten.

Now, I know you want to continue, and I'm anxious for you to. But, you should rest now. Close this little book down for a moment and think about a friend you might have accidentally hurt. Or, think about if *you've* been hurt by a friend. It may not have been on purpose. They're probably still looking for you, too, in their own "Invisible Chamber of Dirty Clothes and Secrets."

Chapter 7

The rabbit quietly shouted in the closet, "Come on, tiger! Come on out! The Moths are gone."

The tiger sighed, "I couldn't….I *shouldn't.*"

The lion interrupted with his head bowed, "Oh, tiger, we've been through this before. It was an accident. He didn't mean to leave you lost in the closet. You can come out whenever you want."

"No, this is where he wants me to be. I couldn't. I *shouldn't!*"

"You're foolishly feeling sorry for yourself, you know? You can come out any time you want. But, you'd rather sit there and sigh all the time about how the boy doesn't love you, when you know very well that isn't true."

"But, he's so sick now, he probably wouldn't even remember me…...*sigh.*"

The little bear had long since come out from under the covers and was sitting on the bed next to Jackson, just listening, just watching all the other animals interact.

The tiger pouted, "I'm a failure…I was supposed to remind him to have fun! To be a joy! To be…...I dunno….Lion, I was supposed to be the one that reminded him to have fun, while you were supposed to remind him to be brave, the rabbit does a good job of reminding him to listen and pay attention, and even the elephant is supposed to remind him to remember his studies and stay smart."

Elephant? What elephant, asked the little bear to himself.

"That reminds me," mentioned the tiger, "what's the bear supposed to remind him of anyway?"

The lion replied on the bear's behalf, "We're still trying to figure that out."

"Oh," said the tiger looking at the bear, "well, it's nice to meet you bear. Has he given you a name yet?"

"No," the bear said. "He hasn't given me a name."

"Not even Teddy?"

"Nope."

"Well, whatever you do, don't leave his side. You could end up forgotten in this closet! I know first hand!"

"Oh, Tiger!" Roared the lion frustrated.

Meanwhile, the rabbit was scouring the bedroom looking for the elephant. "*Aha!* Found you! I found him everyone. He's fine. He's over here behind this chest."

"Of course, I'm fine," chimed the elephant. "I was just reading."

"Reading? Then you must have missed everything. Wow! Let me tell you everything that happened. First, this little bear showed up out of nowhere. Then, he and lion had to hide because the Moths came back. The MOTHS! Can you believe that? Then all of a sudden-…"

"Yes, I know all about that," the elephant said without once leaving the pages of the book he was reading. Oh, and you should have seen the way the elephant reads! He tends to be about the same size of a big, proper book, so he can't hold it in his hands. So, he props it up against this enormous chest by the window and scans the pages with his little eyes, sometimes his tusks brushing the pages, and sometimes his trunk sliding across the floor when he gets to the bottom of the page.

"You know everything that happened?"

"Yes, I was listening. I can read and listen. Seems everything is fine now, right? Everything is back to normal. No Moths, tiger still hiding, lion is holding court, the bear is up in the bed without a name, and I'm reading a book."

"Oh....Ok. Well, I guess that sums it up...."

Tiger interrupted from his woeful place in the closet. "We should be thinking about what to do about the Moths. They'll be back, you know. And we'll all be doomed. *DOOMED!*"

The little bear asked where the Moths came from. The rabbit pointed towards the open window. "They come from out there. Through the window. I do so wish they would close that window!"

"They'd still find a way in," remarked the lion, "they always do."

The little bear stood on the absolute tips of his paws and peeked as far as he could from the bed.

The lion suggested, "Maybe you could just walk over and take a look?"

"Are you sure it's ok? I mean, I don't want to leave him."

"He's fast asleep. Which is best for him right now. Why don't you take a quick trip to the window and take a look."

The little bear reluctantly crawled down the sheets, plopped to the floor and scurried over to the chest by the window. Crawling up the chest he said quite sternly, "I want to hurry and get back to him, in case he needs me."

"I understand," said the lion.

But, what the little bear saw out the window was harder to leave than he may have known.

You see, from atop the chest he could see clearly out of the window a beautiful meadow drenched in sunlight, covered with different sorts of wildflowers, all born of different colors and shapes, some with only a few petals, some with a lot, some with long stems that made them tall, others that sat quietly near the grass. It was so beautiful to the little bear.

"WOW! Have the rest of you seen this????
What is this?"

"That," said the elephant with a very well
informed tone, "is the world."

All was brightly lit by the haze of the sun, the
petals of the flowers, the birds that bounced around
the grass, all swayed a slight bit with a touch of
breeze that moved the air.

"The world is so beautiful! Look at it!
Wow....." The little bear lifted his muzzle and
closed his eyes so he could smell the faint fragrance
of the flowers drift through the air. "Can we go out

there? Maybe something out there can make the boy better! Come on! Let's go!"

And all stuffed animals in attendance screamed all at the same time, "NO!"

The little bear was shocked. "Well, why not? Just looking at it makes *ME* feel better, couldn't it do something for the boy?"

The rabbit said, "You're never to go out there on your own. Never ever never ever, no!"

"Yeah," said the tiger, "you'll end up forgotten....like me."

"Oh, really, tiger. Little bear, we only go out there with the boy. Those are the rules. Tiger is only partly right. If you we go out alone, you could get stuck. Then the Moths will definitely get you, if the rain doesn't first. So, we always go with the boy."

The little bear sighed with a heavy sadness. "I understand. I just....I just wanted to do *something* for him."

"And I agree," said the lion before addressing the other animals. "Instead of worrying about the Moths, we should worry about the boy. We need to get him better."

And of course, tiger had to say something about this. "Well, if the Moths get us first, then we won't *BE* here to help the boy."

The lion had to admit that tiger was also right. They had to figure out what to do about helping Jackson get better, while saving themselves from the Moths.

There was silence for a moment, while they all lowered their heads in deep thought.

This was a tricky situation. Do they help their friend in need, while risking their own safety? Or do they save themselves first and help Jackson later? It's a very difficult situation. I mean, what would you do if you were put in that moment where you had to decide?

All the little animals sat quietly, none of them looking at each other, just looking at the floor....

No one knew what to do.....not even the little bear who wanted to do *something*.

Chapter 8

The door began to open. *Plunk* went all the stuffed animals, right where they were, dropping right there to the floor where they remained motionless.

Dad walked in saying, "I think having a friend visit would be a good idea. He's been sleeping so much."

In walked Dad with a young boy carrying the strangest thing in his hands. Now, I know you want me to *tell* you what it is, but I truly can't. Not even *I* know if it was an animal, or even a monster. It was just this strange stuffed thing that the other stuffed toys in Jackson's room had never seen.

To begin with, he was purple. Not that being purple matters all that much, but it is a fact that it was purple and had the wildest button eyes, and a floppy mane of hair. It didn't look like anything that you could describe.

He was clutched under the arm of Jackson's friend Phillip. And the creature just stared boldly at all the animals on the floor with his big round eyes. The animals looked at each other curiously, except for rabbit, who is always being in need of information to spread, asked with a whisper under his breath, "What in the world is *THAT?*"

Dad tenderly woke Jackson. "Son? Son, can you wake up? You have a visitor. Your friend Phillip is here to see you."

Jackson lifted his head and smiled. He hadn't been to school in so long, hadn't played in the meadow with his friends, hadn't built forts in the woods. Jackson was so happy to see Phillip.

But suddenly, Jackson's face dropped and his eyes went wide, as he started scrambling through his sheets with hectic speed asking, "Dad? Where's my bear? Where's my bear???"

Dad scanned the room with his eyes quickly and said, "Calm down, son. He's over here on the floor." Dad picked up the little bear and handed him to Jackson, who squeezed the little bear so tight.

"I thought I had lost you," he whispered in the bear's ear. "I really thought I had lost you." And what warmth that was, how great that felt to the little bear. When some squeezes can hurt, others can feel so good and so kind, and this hug made the little bear stop thinking so much about what he could do to help Jackson, but just lay there in the boy's arms and enjoy being hugged.

Dad said, "Maybe you could use some fresh air. Would you and Phillip like to go outside?"

"Yeah, Jackson, come outside with me," Phillip said. "We sure do miss you at school. Everyone says building our fort in the woods isn't as much fun without you there. No one can help build a fort like you can."

Dad and Phillip helped Jackson out of bed, helped him put on a robe, and helped him find his slippers, asking the whole time, "Can I take my bear outside?"

Yes! Here is my chance! I get to go outside and see the world, the little bear thought.

Dad said, "I think we'll leave the bear here on the bed so he doesn't get dirty. That way he can keep the bed warm for you."

I don't get to go outside? But, there could be something out there I can find to help the boy! Bears are good at foraging!

Jackson tucked his little knit bear under the covers, laying the bear's head on a pillow. Phillip piped up and said he would leave his stuffed creature there, too, to keep the bear company.

As the two boys went outside to enjoy the fresh air, the little bear *humphed* where he lay, so very disappointed he wasn't able to go outside.

As the little bear turned slowly to the left he saw those big button eyes of the creature beside him. Now, they weren't just button eyes, but different colored buttons, with smaller buttons inside larger buttons.

"Hi. I'm one of Phillip's strange friends," said the purple, button eyed thing.

"You're a what?"

"One of Phillip's strange friends. There are a lot of us. None of us look alike, you know. None of us look like anyone, not even each other. We're all unique."

"You're all different?"

"No, we are all *unique.*"

"What's the difference?"

"Being different just means you're not like everyone else. Being unique means there is something *special* about you."

The elephant asked, "Does that mean you're better?"

"Nope. Just means there's something special about me."

"Like the glitter in your hair?" Asked the rabbit.

"Sure."

The lion growled softly under his mane, "All of us are unique."

"Right! Everyone has something special about them that makes them unique."

And the little bear lowered his head in sadness. "I haven't figured out what makes me unique yet."

"Well, what's your name?"

The little bear sighed, "I don't have one yet. I thought I was here to help take care of the boy, but I guess I'm not even allowed to go outside."

"Oh....Well, if it makes you feel better, I don't have a name either."

"You don't?"

"Nope."

"But, don't you need a name?"

"I don't know. Do you want people to remember you by your name or something special that you've done?"

The bear had nothing to say. Maybe that's true. Maybe we don't need to be known for our names, but rather what we've done that was important, or helpful.

The little bear said, "I really *WANT* to do something special for Jackson. I feel like I want to help him get better so much. *Sooo* much. It's all I think about."

The little bear then jumped off the bed, sauntered across the room and climbed the chest to look out the window where he saw Jackson sitting with Phillip in the grass, little wildflowers all around them, the sun making all of their colors brighter than ever.

"I just don't know what it is I'm supposed to do…. Look at him….."

All of the stuffed animals climbed onto the chest so they could spy out the window and watch Jackson sitting in the sun...even the tiger left the dreary confines of the closet to join them.

"He's such a good boy," said the tiger.

"So sad to see him so sick," replied the lion.

"This is a good day for him. He's smiling, enjoying the sunshine, having fun with his friend," noticed the rabbit.

And they all sat silent again, just watching the boy they cared for so much, all anxiously worrying about what to do to help him. Each of them left alone with their own thoughts.

Now, I could tell you what each of them was thinking, but that wouldn't be fair, would it? Thoughts are private things, unless you decide to share them. Those little stuffed friends in the room all were quiet. Some of them thinking about how much they really loved Jackson and hated to see him suffer. And some of them were still thinking about the Moths…..

CHapter 9

The lion was the first to break the silence and speak up. "We have to do something about the Moths...."

They all knew the lion was right. They all knew that there is nothing than they can do to help Jackson, but even if they could, what use would it be if they were attacked by the Moths?

"Little bear, I want to tell you why you mean so much to the boy."

And there was first a wince, then a hush from the other animals.

"Are you going to tell him about the other bear," asked the rabbit?

The lion said firmly, "Yes, I am."

"Oh, no. I try to forget about it," said the elephant, "but no matter what I do, I never forget anything. I'm going to go read my book."

The tiger said, "I'm going back to the closet. This story makes me sad. Really sad, truly sad, sadder than….sadder than being in that closet, but I just can't hear about it again."

Phillip's strange friend asked, "Did something bad happen?"

"Yes, yes something did."

And the lion began to tell the little bear how he wasn't the first little bear to be there at all, about how another bear had been there first, and how all the other animals had come later.

"That first bear," said the lion, "was so adored by Jackson, so loved by him. All of us loved him. Whenever one of us would arrive, that first bear made us all feel so welcomed. He was such a good friend."

"Such a good friend," repeated the tiger.

The lion continued. "Then one day the Moths came. None of us knew what they were. As a matter of fact, we all found them rather pretty the way they flew in the sunlight. We had no idea they were so dangerous. That first bear was the first to understand, though. At first they just nipped at him. He was scarred, but not too harmed. But, that's when the rest of us realized how dangerous the Moths had become. You see, little bear, the tiger was always in the closet, the elephant was always by the chest reading a book, the rabbit was always rushing about telling stories, and I just sat regally in a corner keeping everything in order. The Moths never really noticed us.

"But, Jackson's first bear never left Jackson side once he got sick, always sat on the bed, snuggled up to the boy in plain sight. At first the moths came only in small numbers. But, one day, the moths came in a fury, flying through the window in such large numbers that you couldn't even see your paw in front of your face.

"The rest of us ran for cover, hiding under sheets and clothes that had been tossed on the floor, jumping under the bed, or rushing to the closet, but that bear, so determined to stay by poor Jackson's side while he was ill, was utterly shredded by the Moths."

The elephant whimpered, "I hate this part of the story."

Again, the lion continued. "Jackson's bear had been destroyed by the Moths. His stuffing had come out, one of his eyes had come undone, his ears had been chewed away, and even one of his paws was about to fall off. He just sat there motionless, his spirit gone, nothing left of him but....wool and stuffing. He never fought them off, nor could he have if he had wanted to. He remained dutiful and stayed by the boy's side despite what it was doing to him. We lost a very dear friend to the Moths, little bear."

"A very dear friend," reminded the rabbit.

The little bear lowered his eyes to the ground, then sat there in a sad crumble. "So, if I'm going to have a purpose, then it's just to be with him all the time....even when the Moths come back? To never leave his side? Is what happened to the other bear what's going to happen to me?"

"You are here to be with the boy, no matter what happens," declared the lion. "No matter what."

There was a sudden wailing from the bed. Phillip's strange friend had just started bawling wildly, "Oh, it's so sad! *SOOO SAD!* Such a sad story! And to think, I just met a new friend and he's....he's....oh, he's going to have to be taken by the Moths just to save the boy! *Sooooo SAD!* Come here, little bear! *COME HERE! Boo hoo hoo hooo!*"

The lion said, "You should go back to the bed anyway. The boy will be back soon."

The little bear climbed into the bed where Phillip's strange friend met him with a quick hug.

"You poor thing! Oh, to think what you'll have to endure!"

"I'll be brave," said the little bear. "I mean, if that's why I'm here, then….well, at least I know now right?"

"I guess that's one way to look at it," said the strange friend with his huge purple, button eyes. "You're so brave, little bear."

The two boys returned, Jackson said his goodbye's to Phillip, the strange friend was collected, and once Jackson had fallen back to sleep, the little bear snuggled up against him feeling brave, yes….but, also feeling very terrified.

CHapter 10

The little bear turned to the boy, saw his sad face, his weak little body, the sweat on his forehead, the boy breathing heavy with a rasp. All night long the little bear had thought about purpose and bravery. He thought about staying with the boy at all times, no matter what should happen. And he did realize quite simply that sometimes being brave can scare you. However, if being brave means saving a friend, then so be it.

"Then so be it," said the little bear courageously. "I can do it, I know I can do it. I can be brave. He needs me, he needs to hold me, to keep me close, and I shall never stray from that. I am brave!"

And from the dark the lion roared tenderly, "Would all animals please come to the center of the room?"

From the elephant, to the rabbit, to the tiger, they all stood in a huddle with apprehension, with worry about what the lion might suggest.

"The bear has it correct," the lion said. "How could we have questioned ourselves for even a moment? It is what we are to do. Our mission has always been to be here for that young boy no matter what. We were never supposed to cower in closets, thinking of ourselves, we were never to land our eyes constantly in books and forget about him, we were never to dash around the room spreading gossip, leaving him unattended. Our jobs were put clear to us the moment he accepted us into his life and showed us love: to be with him always, despite what might happen to us. Now, we will all, I tell you, *ALL* of us climb into that bed with the little bear and do our duty: comforting that boy!"

All those confused, knit animals all turned to each with wide eyes and fear....but also with embarrassment.

The elephant was the first to say, "I feel so ashamed. I was so interested in the book I was reading that I completely forgot about him. I thought he would just get better! I really thought one day he'd just wake up feeling back to normal. I feel terrible. I really do. You're right, lion. I'm in, I'll be brave."

"I was so busy running around and running my mouth," said the rabbit, "that I didn't stop for a moment to check on him. I was so worried and busy about what everyone else was doing that I didn't even stop to think how *the boy* was doing. Count me in, too. I'll be brave."

Now, they all turned to the tiger who said, "But, the Moths....they're coming back! They're going to shred us to pieces! You saw what happened to that other bear! He was massacred!"

But, then the tiger, for the first time in a long time really saw how bad Jackson's illness had gotten. He asked, "What's that sound?"

"That's his breathing," said the lion.

"But, it can't be....it sounds like a gurgle.... Why is he so pale?"

The elephant sadly and ashamedly said, "Because he's ill, tiger. But I guess you had forgotten that. I guess we *all* had."

"But, won't he get better? Isn't he getting any better? I mean, he went outside today to play with his friend, didn't he?"

The rabbit snickered, "You've been in that closet so long you don't know even know what *playing* looks like. He was too weak to move, tiger! He just sat there trying to breathe in fresh air!"

"It is quite interesting," the lion commented, "that we were all so concerned about saving ourselves for fear of not being here for the boy. But, what if something *does* happen to him and he's gone? We won't have anyone to be here for. What would happen to us then? We could be separated, sent to other homes, or worse... we could be forgotten."

The rabbit blurted, "oh, you're going to make me cry! I don't want to think about that. Oh, why do we have to be in this position???"

The tiger gulped with wide eyes and twitching whiskers, "Do you think it could get that bad? I mean, he can't go! He just can't! I don't want him to go! I want him to stay here, right here with us! And get better! I mean, what if he did? Then we worried all about ourselves for nothing. We saved ourselves and let him suffer...."

"You said it yourself, tiger. You want him to be here for us....but, are we here for him?" The lion could be very persuasive.

Finally the tiger understood everything. "I can't believe I've acted this way. I was feeling so sorry for myself that I.....I never took a moment to feel sorry for him."

The tiger rushed to the bed, climbed his way up and sat beside Jackson. "Forgive me, my friend. I'm so sorry I left you alone. Please forgive me. Whatever it takes to make you better, I'll do it. I'll do anything, just…please don't go."

The elephant, tiger, and rabbit all quickly scrambled up the sheets to find a special spot near the boy, while the bear slowly snuggled under the boy's arms, just where he should be and whispered to himself, "I'll be brave…."

And there the animals stayed the entire evening, thinking of nothing else but Jackson….They didn't even think about the Moths.

CHapter 11

The sunlight began dim, just a thin and dainty beam of soft light entering through the window. Slowly, the light got brighter, and the beautiful glow of morning filled the room. The knit animals stirred softly, yawning and stretching, peeking through their eyelids at the new day before them.

"That was the best night's sleep I have had in a long time," said the rabbit. "I had forgotten how nice it was to cuddle beside him."

They all smiled, stood and shook to wake themselves, then sat crouched beside Jackson....that is, all except for the tiger, who sat quiet, eyes closed, head down.

The elephant asked the tiger if he was alright.

"Yes, I'm fine," he said. "I'm wishing for him to get better."

The lion respectfully nodded and said, "Wishing is just what we need. This is just what he needs. This right here, all of us with him together….wishing he will get better."

The bear was awake, too, but did not rustle and get up from the comforting clutch of the boy's hold. He just smiled. And do you know why he smiled? Because all the love and compassion that was in that room will do that to you. Feeling good about helping others, and being there for them, will make you feel so good that you have no choice but to smile. Now, you can do your best not to smile. You could look away, you can think about other things, but something about loving someone and making them feel better will always make your heart smile….and you just can't stop no matter how much you may want to.

"Friends," said the lion, "no matter what happens, I'm glad to know that we are all here together for the sake of this boy, this friend of ours who needs us. I'd like to say that I think this morning proves something about us that we had forgotten. That we are all of us, including the boy, a family. We will be there for each other when times are tough, and if need be, sacrifice to save those we care for."

"I think I'm going to cry again," whispered the tiger, "but don't worry (sniff sniff), it's a happy cry."

"Those are the best kind of cries," replied the elephant. "We could use more of those these days, couldn't we?"

"Now, now, let's not all get weepy," the lion said stoically. "Let's smile knowing we have each other and that Jackson has us to help him!"

The rabbit mentioned what a beautiful morning it was. "Look at how pretty and bright everything is! Look how the sun makes all the colors look so much prettier!"

"Rabbit…." The lion was quietly begging for the rabbit's attention. "Rabbit…don't move."

"Oh, I don't want to move, I want to sit here all day with the boy and just enjoy the sunlight."

"Rabbit, please sit quietly."

"But, why shouldn't I say how beautiful a day it will be? And why are all of you looking at me like that?"

What the rabbit didn't know was that there was one singular little Moth floating around his head. It didn't move quickly, didn't dash rapidly, it just hovered quietly and slowly around the rabbit's ears, and not one of the animals had seen it flitter through the sunbeams, for the Moth simply glided in soundlessly, unseen, undetected.

The elephant just point above the rabbit's ears and whispered as low as he could, "*M-m-m-mothhhhh!!!!*"

Struck with panic the rabbit stuttered to ask, "What should I do???"

"I don't know," said the lion.

That one Moth softly glided here, then glided there.....then stopped in midair. For just a moment it seemed to be disinterested in the rabbit's wool ears. But, then? *BAM!* Out of nowhere he started buzzing with a *flappptiy fllmphht fllapp flapp!* That was the signal, that was the code! That signaled the invasion!

The lion looked quickly towards the window. "Oh, no. There are more of them! Many more!"

Swarming through the room was a squadron of Moths, all of them in different sizes, all quickly floating in random patterns through the air, searching for the knit animals, attracted to that unique scent of wool, massive amounts of them, more than you can count stars in the sky.

The animals began to quiver with fear, clutching at each other, swatting away the swarm that had now started a full attack. The Moths zinged through the air, striking hard and fast, nibbling at the rabbit's ears, biting at the lion's cheek, with the tiger and elephant also being gnawed at by the atrocious bugs.

Their wings were swift, their siege was sharp, and the animals shouldered together, holding each other closely while still trying to swat away the little demons. There were so many of them! *Too* many of them to fight off, and still they kept pouring in through the window, through the sunbeams that lit up the dust in the air!

A few Moths were pulling out the tiger's whiskers, and a few more were chewing at the lion's tale. And no matter what the animals did to fight them off, the Moths were winning!

But, what about the little bear? He saw what was happening, his family being harmed and hurt, destroyed and unable to fight back…but apparently, the Moths did not even notice the little bear. They weren't attacking him, weren't chewing on him. Should he stay under the covers and save himself? Surely, not! They were not only friends, they were his family! And they were going to stick together no matter what!

"Come here!" Shouted the little bear through the flying madness of Moths that enveloped them. "Come here! Under the boys arms! We'll do this together! You go under his arms, I'll stand up front!"

The animals scurried quickly to where the bear had been nestled under Jackson's arm, the Moths following them, never letting go. This sad pile of knit animals coward bravely under the boys arms, each holding onto each other, with the teddy bear up front, protecting his friends.

He would let himself be taken by the Moths, he would save his friends and there was nothing anyone could do about it. It was his purpose! And perhaps if the Moths were able to overtake the bear, then maybe they'd be too hungry to attack the other animals.

"Lay down behind me," he shouted to his friends. And there they all lay, hiding from the stings of the Moths, under Jackson's arm, behind the little bear. That little bear stood proudly as a fortress, willing to let himself to be taken by the Moths to save his family, but also, to keep his promise to never leave the boy's side.

But, the most peculiar thing happen. The Moths didn't bite at the little bear. No, as a matter of fact, they ignored him all together. It was as if the little bear didn't even exist to the Moths. They acted like he wasn't even there! The little bear swat at them, fought them, yelled at them to go, but they acted as if he were nothing to them, as though he didn't even exist! Which angered the little bear so!

"I will not let you hurt my family! I'm here to take, but not them! I'm brave!"

And slowly, they started drifting away, quite furiously, you know, for the Moths were sure that wool had been here before.

"I don't understand," whispered the lion. "They're leaving….Why aren't they biting you?"

"I don't know!"

And one by one the dangerous little Moths flew out the window, mad dashing back to the bed to double check, then flying out the window. Soon, there were no Moths left at all.

That was it. That was simply it. They were gone. And everyone was confused.

"I think they're gone," the bear said.

The animals slowly came out from under Jackson's arm, from out of the covers, to simply sit and stare at the little bear in amazement.

The tiger asked, "How did you do that? Do you have magical powers?"

"I don't know! They just acted like they didn't see me. And you were so well hidden behind me, they didn't even see you!"

Then the lion began to realize something, something he had suspected, but didn't realize until Phillip's strange friend had started talking about being unique. The lion moved closer to the bear and lifted his head high, "I think I know how you managed to save us little bear, how you saved us all. You are indeed unique." And the lion smiled.

The little bear was so confused. "I don't understand. How?"

"Don't you understand," the lion remarked with reverence for the little bear, "that you are different from us. You are unique. Obviously, you are *not made of wool*."

Indeed, the lion was correct. After what had happened to the first bear, Dad had decided never to make another toy for Jackson out of wool again. He used a material that looked like wool, and felt like wool, but wasn't wool at all.

"I'm not made of wool?"

"No, you are not, my friend. So, the Moths couldn't even tell you were here. You were of no concern to them. You were practically invisible. You are very definitely here for a reason. So that the boy would never lose another bear to the Moths again."

And the lion bowed his head to show his gratitude. All the animals patted the little bear on the back and thanked him with all the sincerity that is possible.

The little bear was in shock. But, you would think his bravery was so simple, right? I mean, after all, he wouldn't have been hurt by the Moths anyway, considering he wasn't made of wool. But, the little bear didn't know that. And neither did the other animals. It is *intention* that matters.

Never forget, the little bear was going to let the Moths destroy him in order to save his friends, and that is what he remembered first and foremost. All he had to do was simply *be there* for them in order to save them. If he had not decided to risk himself, surely, all of his friends would have perished.

You see, my young friend, sometimes bravery is very grand like risking yourself to help another. But, sometimes bravery can be very simple, just being there to love someone is very brave, just being there to comfort them can be very brave. Indeed, this little bear was very brave for a very simple reason: he was there for his friends when they needed him.

Suddenly, the door began to open and all the animals fell into place on the bed, as though they had been discarded there, dropped from the sky, limp and lovely.

In walked Jackson's Mom who immediately saw her son in such a state of illness that she sat on the bed next to him and began to weep.

Jackson's eyes sluggishly began to open. "Mom? Is that you?"

"Yes, it's me, sweetheart! Give me a hug please, I sure could use it."

That was the tightest hug anyone in the world has ever experienced. "I'm so sorry, Mom! I'm so sorry!"

"For what?"

"For hurting your feelings!"

"Don't you worry about that. Don't you worry about that at all. I want you to worry about getting better."

Mom didn't want to stop hugging Jackson. She kept her grip firm on him and rocked him back and forth saying, "You just get better for me, ok? You just get better. I came to stay with you in case you need anything at all from me to make you feel better, ok?"

And Jackson whispered, "This is all I ever needed. Do you forgive me, Mom?"

"There is nothing to forgive, sweetheart….Everything is going to be ok."

Chapter 12

In the days that followed Jackson got better and better. He started getting his strength back, started eating more, and even started laughing out loud at some of his comic books.

Now that Jackson was getting well again, his Mom was helping him tidy up his room. As she picked up the rabbit she said, "Jackson, the Moths are going to get hold of your animal friends again if you don't put them away. This poor little thing has bites on his ears. Now, your father built you a very nice cedar chest to keep them safe when you're not here to protect them. So, you should learn to put your toys away to keep them safe."

And the animals looked at each other stunned.

"I'm sorry, Mom. I just forget sometimes."

"Well, you need to be more careful with your animal friends. They're here to protect you, so you

should respect them for that, and protect them, too."
Then she said with a smile, "Start putting your toys
away, young man," and kissed him on the cheek.

Mom picked up the rabbit, then the elephant,
the lion and tiger and put them in the cedar chest
that Dad had made for Jackson quite sometime
before. Yes, the very chest that sat by the window
that all the animals stood on to watch Jackson play
outside was the very sanctuary that had been made
to protect them from the Moths. Dad was a very
clever man. Moths cannot stand the smell of cedar.
They hate the smell of cedar and will fly away
quickly if they go anywhere near it.

With the animals inside the chest, and the lid
closed behind, the tiger said, "You mean we could
have been protected all this time? And we didn't
know????"

"I guess so," said the lion. "But, at least now
we know what to do next time the Moths come. We

have a fortress to hide in!" And all the animals gleefully smiled. "We'll be safe from now on."

And sure enough, after that the animals would spend all of their time with Jackson when he was in the bedroom, but before he left to go out, he would place his animal friends kindly in the cedar chest and say, "Be safe! I'll be back later!"

Most nights, he let them sleep in bed with him. Now, the animals would all stick together, with each of them taking turns to keep a look out for the Moths, and when they would see the slightest hint of a Moth, they would nudge each other, say, "Let's go!" and dash into the cedar chest, coming back out when the coast was clear, and snuggle up next to Jackson.

And after seeing how ill Jackson had become, and so grateful that he was now getting better, Mom realized how very unimportant all the dashing around the city was. The life of running about to look important no longer interested her. She began to realize the simple treasures in life, the most important of those treasures being Jackson. So, she decided to move out to the woods to be close to Dad and Jackson again, and all three were once again a very happy family.

Soon Jackson was able to go outside again, run through the woods, jump through the meadow and leap over the creek with his friends. Sometimes he took his little bear with him. And the little bear got to see the outside world, see the forest and the big trees, feel the flowers as they grazed his cheek as Jackson sat in the grass.

One day Jackson and the little bear were sitting alone beside a very large tree. Jackson was holding his little bear close to his chest and said, "I know you had so much to do with my getting better. Thank you for being there for me when I needed you. Thank you so much, little bear!"

Then Jackson lifted the bear high in the sky and said, "I'm going to call you... *'The teddy bear that saved me!'*"

Now, there is much more I could say about this story, much more indeed. But, I'm hoping you were able to learn how simple just being there for someone is when they are in need, and how forgetting about yourself sometimes is so very brave.

I'll end the story here, because I do so enjoy when a story ends happily, don't you?

We'll share some time again in the future, little one. Until then....be brave!

THe ENd

Let's KNit!

Would you like to knit your own teddy bear, rabbit, or tiger? In the following pages you will find knitting patterns to help you get started. If you don't know how to knit, perhaps you can find someone to help you, and pretty soon, you'll have your own collection of animals to keep you company!

THe Teddy Bear THat Saved Me

Legs (make 2)

Using 2 double pointed needles cast on 10 stitches, leaving about a 3 inch strand from your slip knot (This will come in handy later).

Beginning at the sole, purl the first row.

Next Row: (right side) k1fb, k1,m1 (7 times) k1, k1fb (19 stitches)

Next Row: purl all stitches

Next Row: k4, m1, [k3, m1] 4 times, k3 (24 stitches)

Work in stockinet stitch for 5 rows

Next Row: k8, [k2tgther 4 times] k8 (20 stitches)

Next Row: purl all stitches

Next Row: k6, [k2tgthr 4 times,] k6 (16 stitches)

Next Row: purl all stitches

Next Row: k7, k2tgthr, k7 (15 stitches) Work in stockinet stitch for 3 rows. Next Row: k2, m1, k11, m1, k2 (17 stitches) Work in stockinet stitch for 15 rows.

Next Row: k1 [k2tgthr 8 times]

Cut yarn leaving a long (about 18") strand, thread through remaining stitches and draw tightly. With rights sides facing, sew up leg seam with long strand, and the sole using the original cast on strand, leaving a small hole at the ankle. Turn inside out, stuff with fiberfill and sew up ankle using the long strand. Set aside for assembly later.

Arms (make 2)

Using 2 double pointed needles cast on 6 stitches, leaving about a 2 inch strand from your slip not for use later.

Beginning at the shoulder, purl the first row.

Next Row: k1fb, [k1, m1 3 times] k1, k1fb (11 stitches)

Next Row: purl all stitches.

Next Row: k2, m1, k2, m1, k3, m1, k2, m1, k2 (15 stitches)

Work in stockinet for 29 rows.

Next Row: k1, [k2tgthr 7 times].

Cut yarn leaving a long (about 18") strand, thread through remaining stitches and draw tightly. With right sides facing, sew up arm seam using long strand and using the 2 inch original cast on thread, sew up shoulder, leaving a small opening (about half an inch) near the top of the arm seam near the shoulder. Turn inside out, stuff with fiberfill and sew up small opening using the long strand. Set aside for assembly later.

Body

Beginning at the bottom of the body and with double pointed needles cast on 9 stitches. Divide evenly onto three needles. Join, careful not to twist, and knit each stitch. Place marker to denote beginning of round.

First round: k1, k1fb, k1 on each needle. (12 stitches)

Next round: knit each stitch

Next round: k1fb in each stitch around. (24 stitches) Next round: knit each stitch.

Next round: (k3, k1fb) around. (30 stitches) Next round: knit each stitch.

Next round: (k4, k1fb) around. (36 stitches) Next round: knit each stitch.

Next round: (k5, k1fb) around. (42 stitches) Next round: knit each stitch.

Next round: (k6, k1fb) around. (48 stitches) Next round: knit each stitch.

Next round: (k7, k1fb) around. (54 stitches) Knit 20 rounds.

Next round: (k7, k2tog) around. (48 stitches) Next round: knit each stitch.

Next round: (k6, k2tog) around. (42 stitches) Next round: knit each stitch.

Next round: (k5, k2tog) around. (36 stitches) Next round: knit each stitch.

Next round: (k4, k2tog) around. (30 stitches) Next round: knit each stitch.

Next round: (k3, k2tog) around. (24 stitches) Next round: knit each stitch.

Next round: (k2, k2tog) around. (18 stitches) Next round: knit each stitch.

Next round. k2tog around. (9 stitches)

Cut yarn, leaving a long strand (about 18") and thread through live stitches and pull off needle, but do NOT draw through yet!

Sew up cast on hole with cast on strand from the inside. Stuff firmly with fiberfill, then draw long strand tightly, closing up hole. Sew up hole with 2 or 3 stitches to securely close the body. Leave long strand, set aside later for assembly.

Head

Beginning at muzzle and with double pointed needles cast on 9 stitches. Divide evenly onto three needles. Join, careful not to twist, and knit each stitch. Place marker to denote beginning of round.

First round: k1, k1fb, k1 on each needle. (12 stitches)

Next round: knit each stitch

Next round: k1fb in each stitch around. (24 stitches) Knit three rounds.

Next round: (k3, k1fb) around. (30 stitches) Knit three rounds.

Next round: (k4, k1fb) around. (36 stitches) Knit two rounds.

Next round: (k5, k1fb) around. (42 stitches) Next round: knit each stitch.

Next round: (k6, k1fb) around. (48 stitches) Knit 10 rounds.

Next round: (k6, k2tog) around. (42 stitches) Next round: knit each stitch.

Next round: (k5, k2tog) around. (36 stitches) Next round: knit each stitch.

Next round: (k4, k2tog) around. (30 stitches) Next round: knit each stitch.

Next round: (k3, k2tog) around. (24 stitches) Next round: knit each stitch.

Next round: (k2, k2tog) around. (18 stitches) Next round: knit each stitch.

Next round. k2tog around. (9 stitches)

Cut yarn, leaving a long strand (about 18") and thread through live stitches and pull off needle, but do NOT draw through yet!

Sew up muzzle with cast on strand from the inside. Stuff firmly with fiberfill, then draw long strand tightly, closing up hole at the back of the head. Sew up hole with 2 or 3 stitches to securely close. Leave long strand, set aside for assembly later.

Ears (make 2)

With 2 double pointed needles, cast on 6 stitches.

First row: k1fb in each stitch.

Next row: purl each stitch.

Next row: (k1, k1fb) across. Next row: purl each stitch.

Next row: (k2, k1fb) across.

Work stockinet for 3 rows.

Next row: (k2, k2tog) across. Next row: purl each stitch.

Next row: (k1, k2tog) across.

Next row: purl each stitch.

Next row: k2tog across.

Cut yarn leaving long strand, thread through remaining stitches on needle and pull tightly.

Assembly

Embroider nose, mouth and eyes. Attach ears to the sides of the head. Attach body to head using the long strand. For the legs, pull long strand up through bottom of soul and bring up to the top of the piece for assembly. For the arms, make sure the seam side faces the back of the bear, drawing long strand to either side of the piece to make sure the seam faces the back.

TIGERS ARE FOR CUDDLING

One skein each of Paton's Classic Wool in Aran, Pumpkin, and Black

One set of 4 Double Pointed needles size 4 (sounds much smaller than the needle recommended for this yarn, but this needle size works best).

Polyester Fiberfill

Small amount (about 2 yards) of black wool for the eyes and nose.

Small crochet hook for whiskers

Helpful abbreviations: k1fb=knit one stitch front and back

m1=make one stitch between current stitch and next stitch k2tog=knit two stitches together (No gauge required for this pattern

This tiger is worked up in individual pieces, leaving a long strand at both casting on and casting off to help with easy sewing.

Legs (make 2)

Using 2 double pointed needles and aran cast on 10 stitches, leaving about a 3 inch strand from your slip knot (This will come in handy later).

Beginning at the sole, purl the first row.

Next Row: (right side) k1fb, [k1,m1] (7 times) k1, k1fb (19 stitches)

Next Row: purl all stitches

Next Row: k4, m1, [k3, m1] 4 times, k3 (24 stitches)

Work in stockinet stitch for 5 rows

Switch to black

Next Row: k8, [k2tgther 4 times] k8 (20 stitches)

Next Row: purl all stitches

Switch to pumpkin (alternate between black and pumpkin every two rows, switching colors on the right side of the work until the end).

Next Row: k6, [k2tgthr 4 times,] k6 (16 stitches)

Next Row: purl all stitches

Next Row: k7, k2tgthr, k7 (15 stitches)

Work in stockinet stitch for 3 rows. Next Row: k2, m1, k11, m1, k2 (17 stitches) Work in stockinet stitch for 15 rows.

Next Row: k1 [k2tgthr 8 times]

Cut yarn leaving a long (about 18") strand, thread through remaining stitches and draw tightly. With rights sides facing, tie up loose yarn from other colors, sew up leg seam with long strand, and the sole using the original cast on strand, leaving a small hole at the ankle. Turn inside out, stuff with fiberfill and sew up ankle using the long strand. Set aside for assembly later.

Arms (make 2)

Using 2 double pointed needles and pumpkin cast on 6 stitches, leaving about a 2 inch strand from your slip not for use later.

Beginning at the shoulder, purl the first row.

Next Row: k1fb, [k1, m1 3 times] k1, k1fb (11 stitches)

Switch to black and alternate between black and pumpkin every two rows, switching colors on the right side of the piece until row 26)

Next Row: purl all stitches.

Next Row: k2, m1, k2, m1, k3, m1, k2, m1, k2 (15 stitches) Work in stockinet for 26 rows.

Switch to aran and work in stockinet for 4 more rows.

Next Row: k1, [k2tgthr 7 times].

Cut yarn leaving a long (about 18") strand, thread through remaining stitches and draw tightly. With right sides facing, sew up arm seam using long strand and using the 2 inch original cast on thread, sew up shoulder, leaving a small opening (about half an inch) near the top of the arm seam near the shoulder. Turn inside out, stuff with fiberfill and sew up small opening using the long strand. Set aside for assembly later.

Body

Beginning at the bottom of the body and with double pointed needles and pumpkin cast on 9 stitches. Divide evenly onto three needles. Join, careful not to twist, and knit each stitch. Place marker to denote beginning of round.

First round: k1, k1fb, k1 on each needle. (12 stitches)

Switch to black and alterante between black and pumpkin every two rounds

Next round: knit each stitch

Next round: k1fb in each stitch around. (24 stitches) Next round: knit each stitch.

Next round: (k3, k1fb) around. (30 stitches) Next round: knit each stitch.

Next round: (k4, k1fb) around. (36 stitches) Next round: knit each stitch.

Next round: (k5, k1fb) around. (42 stitches) Next round: knit each stitch.

Next round: (k6, k1fb) around. (48 stitches) Next round: knit each stitch.

Next round: (k7, k1fb) around. (54 stitches) Knit 20 rounds.

Next round: (k7, k2tog) around. (48 stitches) Next round: knit each stitch.

Next round: (k6, k2tog) around. (42 stitches) Next round: knit each stitch.

Next round: (k5, k2tog) around. (36 stitches) Next round: knit each stitch.

Next round: (k4, k2tog) around. (30 stitches) Next round: knit each stitch.

Next round: (k3, k2tog) around. (24 stitches) Next round: knit each stitch.

Next round: (k2, k2tog) around. (18 stitches) Next round: knit each stitch.

Next round. k2tog around. (9 stitches)

Cut yarn, leaving a long strand (about 18") and thread through live stitches and pull off needle, but do NOT draw through yet!

Sew up cast on hole with cast on strand from the inside. Stuff firmly with fiberfill, then draw long strand tightly, closing up hole. Sew up hole with 2 or 3 stitches to securely close the body. Leave long strand, set aside later for assembly.

Head

Beginning at muzzle and with double pointed needles and aran cast on 9 stitches. Divide evenly onto three needles. Join, careful not to twist, and knit each stitch. Place marker to denote beginning of round.

First round: k1, k1fb, k1 on each needle. (12 stitches)

Next round: knit each stitch

Next round: k1fb in each stitch around. (24 stitches) Knit three rounds.

Next round: (k3, k1fb) around. (30 stitches) Knit three rounds.

Switch to pumpkin

Next round: (k4, k1fb) around. (36 stitches) Knit two rounds.

Next round: (k5, k1fb) around. (42 stitches) Next round: knit each stitch.

Next round: (k6, k1fb) around. (48 stitches)

Knit 4 rounds. Switch to black and alternate between black and pumpkin every two rounds. Knit 6 more rounds.

Next round: (k6, k2tog) around. (42 stitches) Next round: knit each stitch.

Next round: (k5, k2tog) around. (36 stitches) Next round: knit each stitch.

Next round: (k4, k2tog) around. (30 stitches) Next round: knit each stitch.

Next round: (k3, k2tog) around. (24 stitches) Next round: knit each stitch.

Next round: (k2, k2tog) around. (18 stitches) Next round: knit each stitch.

Next round. k2tog around. (9 stitches)

Cut yarn, leaving a long strand (about 18") and thread through live stitches and pull off needle, but do NOT draw through yet!

Sew up muzzle with cast on strand from the inside. Stuff firmly with fiberfill, then draw long strand tightly, closing up hole at the back of the head. Sew up hole with 2 or 3 stitches to securely close. Leave long strand, set aside for assembly later.

Ears (make 2)

With 2 double pointed needles and black cast on 6 stitches.

First row: k1fb in each stitch.

Next row: purl each stitch.

Next row: (k1, k1fb) across. Next row: purl each stitch.

Next row: (k1, k2tog) across.

Next row: purl each stitch.

Next row: k2tog across.

Cut yarn leaving long strand, thread through remaining stitches on needle and pull tightly.

Tail

Using 2 double pointed needles and pumpkin cast on 6 stitches, leaving about a 2 inch strand from your slip not for use later.

Beginning at the shoulder, purl the first row.

Next Row: k1fb, [k1, m1 3 times] k1, k1fb (11 stitches)

Switch to black and alternate between black and pumpkin every two rows, switching colors on the right side of the piece.

Work in stockinet for 30 rows.

Switch to aran and work in stockinet for 6 more rows.

Next Row: k1, [k2tgthr 7 times].

Cut yarn leaving a long (about 18") strand, thread through remaining stitches and draw tightly. With right sides facing, sew up arm seam using long strand and using the 2 inch original cast on thread, sew up shoulder, leaving a small opening (about half an inch) near the top of the arm seam near the shoulder. Turn inside out, stuff with fiberfill and sew up small opening using the long strand. Set aside for assembly later.

Whiskers

Cut 6 pieces of aran about 2 inches long. Using fringe technique, add three whiskers to each side, then fray slightly.

Assembly

Embroider nose, mouth and eyes. Attach ears to the sides of the head. Attach body to head using the long strand. For the legs, pull long strand up through bottom of soul and bring up to the top of the piece for assembly. For the arms, make sure the seam side faces the back of the bear, drawing long strand to either side of the piece to make sure the seam faces the back. If you need some help, I have some video tutorials on my blog!

A Little Boy's Bunny

Materials

One skein of Lionbrand Fisherman's Wool in Oatmeal

One skein of Lionbrand Fisherman's Wool in Natural

One set of 4 Double Pointed needles size 5

Polyester Fiberfill

Small amount (about 2 yards) of brown wool for the eyes, nose and mouth.

*This pattern makes up to 3 rabbits.

Helpful abbreviations: k1fb=knit one stitch front and back

m1=make one stitch between current stitch and next stitch

k2tog=knit two stitches together (No gauge required for this pattern)

The rabbit is worked up in individual pieces, leaving a long strand at both casting on and casting off to help with easy sewing.

Legs (make 2)

Using Oatmeal and 2 double pointed needles cast on 10 stitches, leaving about a 3 inch strand from your slip knot (This will come in handy later).

Beginning at the sole, purl the first row.

Next Row: (right side) k1fb, k1,m1 (7 times) k1, k1fb (19 stitches)

Next Row: purl all stitches

Next Row: k4, m1, [k3, m1] 4 times, k3 (24 stitches)

Work in stockinet stitch for 7 rows

Next Row: k8, [k2tgthr 4 times] k8 (20 stitches)

Next Row: purl all stitches

Next Row: k6, [k2tgthr 4 times,] k6 (16 stitches)

Next Row: purl all stitches

Next Row: k7, k2tgthr, k7 (15 stitches) Work in stockinet stitch for 3 rows. Next Row: k2, m1, k11, m1, k2 (17 stitches) Work in stockinet stitch for 25 rows.

Next Row: k1 [k2tgthr 8 times]

Cut yarn leaving a long (about 18") strand, thread through remaining stitches and draw tightly. With rights sides facing, sew up leg seam with long strand, and the sole using the original cast on strand, leaving a small hole at the ankle. Turn inside out, stuff with fiberfill and sew up ankle using the long strand. Set aside for assembly later.

Arms (make 2)

Using Oatmeal and 2 double pointed needles cast on 6 stitches, leaving about a 2 inch strand from your slip not for use later. Beginning at the shoulder, purl the first row.

Next Row: k1fb, [k1, m1 3 times] k1, k1fb (11 stitches) Next Row: purl all stitches.

Next Row: k2, m1, k2, m1, k3, m1, k2, m1, k2 (15 stitches) Work in stockinet for 29 rows.

Next Row: k1, [k2tgthr 7 times].

Cut yarn leaving a long (about 18") strand, thread through remaining stitches and draw tightly. With right sides facing, sew up arm seam using long strand and using the 2 inch original cast on thread, sew up shoulder, leaving a small opening (about half an inch) near the top of the arm seam near the shoulder. Turn inside out, stuff with fiberfill and sew up small opening using the long strand. Set aside for assembly later.

Body

Using Oatmeal and beginning at the bottom of the body and with double pointed needles cast on 9 stitches. Divide evenly onto three needles. Join, careful not to twist, and knit each stitch. Place marker to denote beginning of round. First round: k1, k1fb, k1 on each needle. (12 stitches)

Next round: knit each stitch

Next round: k1fb in each stitch around. (24 stitches) Next round: knit each stitch.

Next round: (k3, k1fb) around. (30 stitches) Next round: knit each stitch.

Next round: (k4, k1fb) around. (36 stitches) Next round: knit each stitch.

Next round: (k5, k1fb) around. (42 stitches) Next round: knit each stitch.

Next round: (k6, k1fb) around. (48 stitches) Next round: knit each stitch. Knit 25 rounds.

Next round: knit each stitch.

Next round: (k6, k2tog) around. (42 stitches) Next round: knit each stitch.

Next round: (k5, k2tog) around. (36 stitches) Next round: knit each stitch.

Next round: (k4, k2tog) around. (30 stitches) Next round: knit each stitch.

Next round: (k3, k2tog) around. (24 stitches) Next round: knit each stitch.

Next round: (k2, k2tog) around. (18 stitches) Next round: knit each stitch.

Next round. k2tog around. (9 stitches)

Cut yarn, leaving a long strand (about 18") and thread through live stitches and pull off needle, but do NOT draw through yet!

Sew up cast on hole with cast on strand from the inside. Stuff firmly with fiberfill, then draw long strand tightly, closing up hole. Sew up hole with 2 or 3 stitches to securely close the body. Leave long strand, set aside later for assembly.

Head

Using Natural and beginning at nose, cast on 9 stitches. Divide evenly onto three needles.

Join, careful not to twist, and knit each stitch. Place marker to denote beginning of round.

First round: k1, k1fb, k1 on each needle. (12 stitches)

Next round: knit each stitch

Next round: k1fb in each stitch around. (24 stitches)

Knit two rounds. Switch to Oatmeal and knit two more rounds. Next round: (k3, k1fb) around. (30 stitches) Knit four rounds.

Next round: (k4, k1fb) around. (36 stitches) Knit three rounds.

Next round: (k5, k1fb) around. (42 stitches) Next round: knit each stitch.

Next round: (k6, k1fb) around. (48 stitches) Knit 10 rounds.

Next round: (k6, k2tog) around. (42 stitches) Next round: knit each stitch.

Next round: (k5, k2tog) around. (36 stitches) Next round: knit each stitch.

Next round: (k4, k2tog) around. (30 stitches) Next round: knit each stitch.

Next round: (k3, k2tog) around. (24 stitches) Next round: knit each stitch.

Next round: (k2, k2tog) around. (18 stitches) Next round: knit each stitch.

Next round. k2tog around. (9 stitches)

Cut yarn, leaving a long strand (about 18") and thread through live stitches and pull off needle, but do NOT draw through yet!

Sew up muzzle with cast on strand from the inside. Stuff firmly with fiberfill, then draw long strand tightly, closing up hole at the back of the head. Sew up hole with 2 or 3 stitches to securely close. Leave long strand, set aside for assembly later.

Ears (make 2)

Using Oatmeal and 2 double pointed needles, cast on 12 stitches.

Work in stockinet stitch for 12 rows.

Next row: knit 2tog at each end of row. (alternate every row) Next row: purl (alternate every other row) Repeat last two rows until one stitch remains.

Cut yarn leaving long strand, thread through last remaining stitch on needle and pull tightly.

Assembly

Embroider nose, mouth and eyes. Attach ears to the sides of the head with right side facing the front of the bunny. Attach body to head using the long strand. For the legs, pull long strand up through bottom of soul and bring up to the top of the piece for assembly. For the arms, make sure the seam side faces the back of the bear, drawing long strand to either side of the piece to make sure the seam faces the back.